MW00874979

Can You Keep A Secret?

Written By: Kimberly P. Truesdale

Illustrated by: Remero Colston

ISBN-13: 978-0-9997284-0-6

To the little girls of the world, may you know that you are all superheroes.

Around the world, boys and girls are pretending to be superheroes.

But if you look closely, you will see five girls who are not pretending.

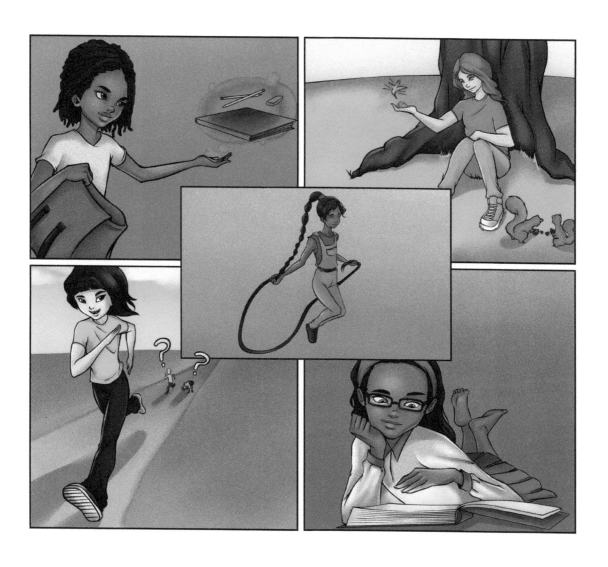

Do you see them? If you do, SSSSH. Don't say anything.

We don't want Kiran to find them. He has been searching the whole universe for these special girls in order to stop them from fulfilling their destiny.

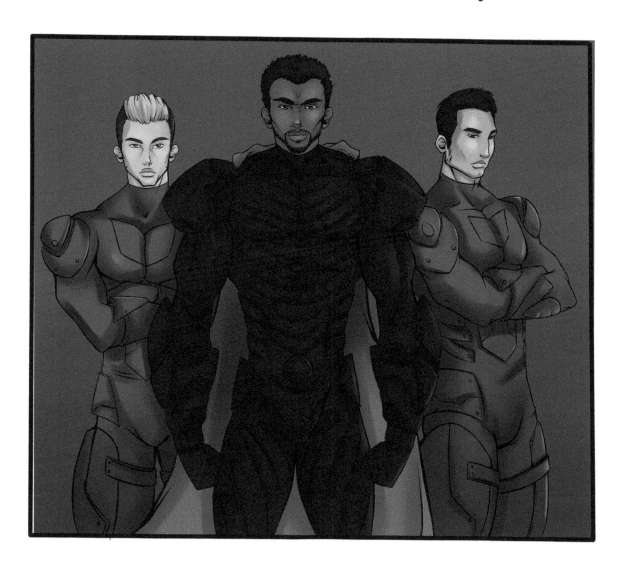

Each girl was sent to a different place on Earth to live. There they will blend in with everyone else and learn to control their powers.

Caribbean Sea
PANAMA
VENEZ.
BOGOTÁ
Galápagos Is.
COLOMBIA
ECUADOR
PERU
BRAZIL
Pacific Ocean
N. Ireland
North Sea
Irish Sea
England
IRELAND
LONDON
Wales
Atlantic Ocean
English Channel
SOUTH CAROLINA
Myrtle Beach
Charleston
GEORGIA
Savannah
Atlantic Ocean
Korean Peninsula
Seoul
South Korea
Jammu-Kashmir
Punjab
Uttar Pradesh
China
Delhi
Agra
Rajasthan
India
Varanasi
Gujarat
Madhya Pradesh
Maharashtra
Mumbai
Orissa
Kolkata
Goa
Andra Pradesh
Karnataka
Madras
Kerala
Tamil Nadu

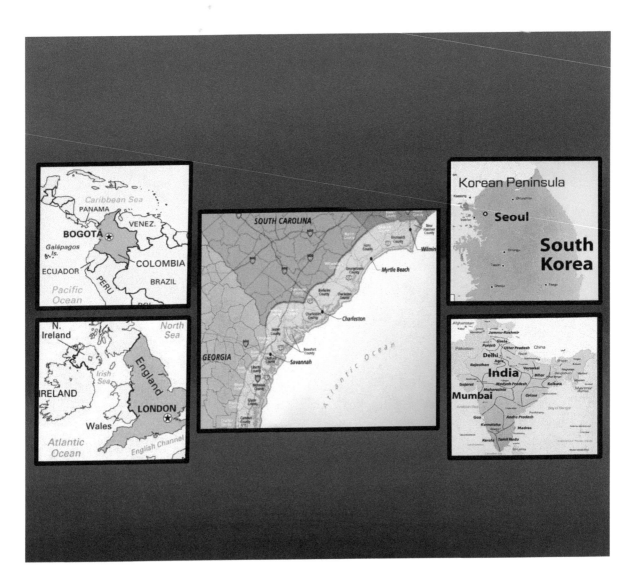

One day, these girls will grow up to be called ***The Keepers***. Their job will be to '*keep*' the universe safe from evil.

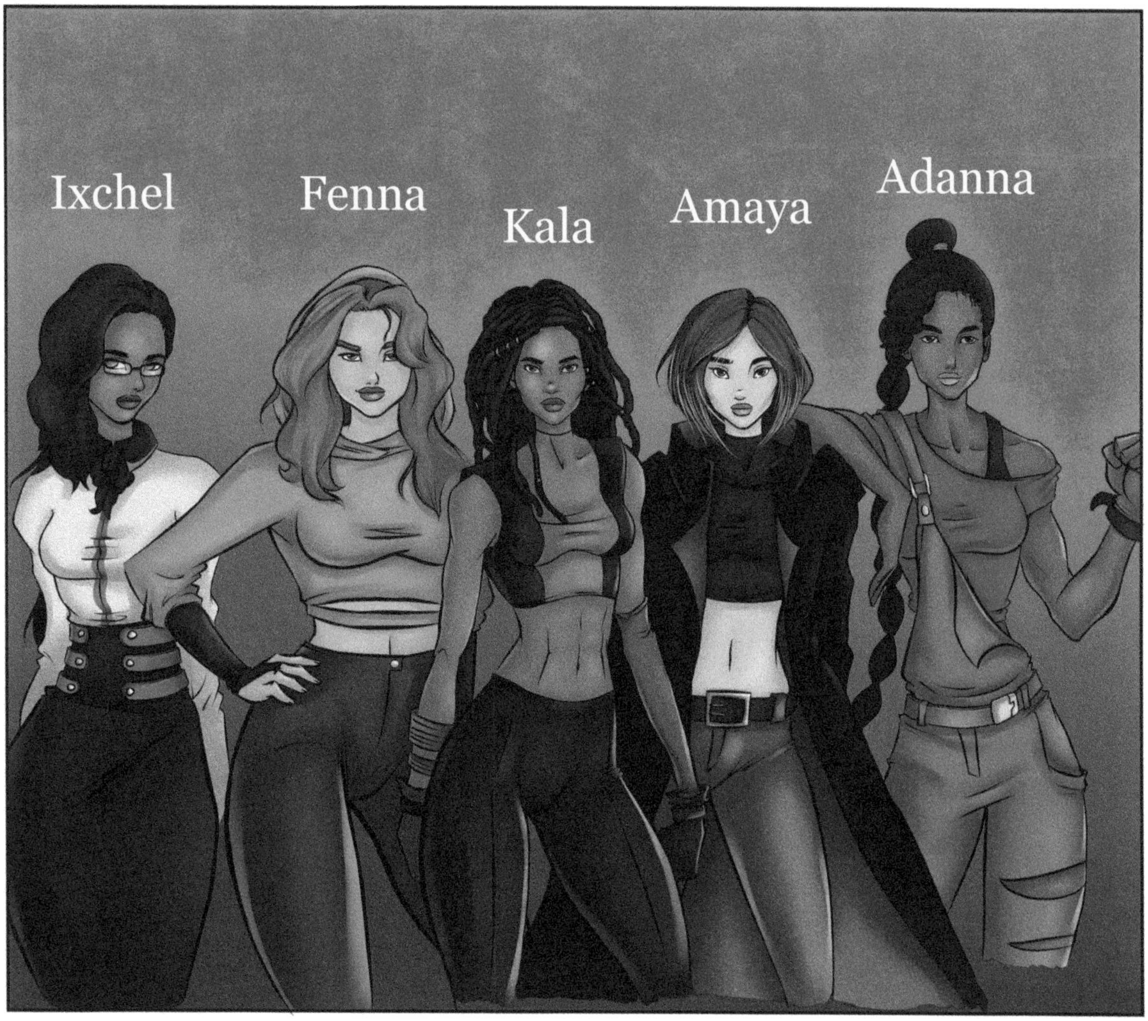
Ixchel
Fenna
Kala
Amaya
Adanna

In Mumbai, India, Adanna stops playing with her toys and looks at the customers coming into her dad's shop. Even in a city of 22 million people, Adanna is happy playing alone —jumping rope with her hair or fixing her toys.

When her toys break, she can change her hand into different tools and fix them. But she can't use her power in front of strangers — only her dad and her auntie know what she can do.

Adanna did show another Keeper, Fenna, her special power when they were on the transport to Earth. "I wonder if she still remembers me," Adanna thought.

Over 4,000 miles away in London, England, Fenna is daydreaming when she accidentally cuts herself. Looking down at her hand, she watches the cut heal on its own.

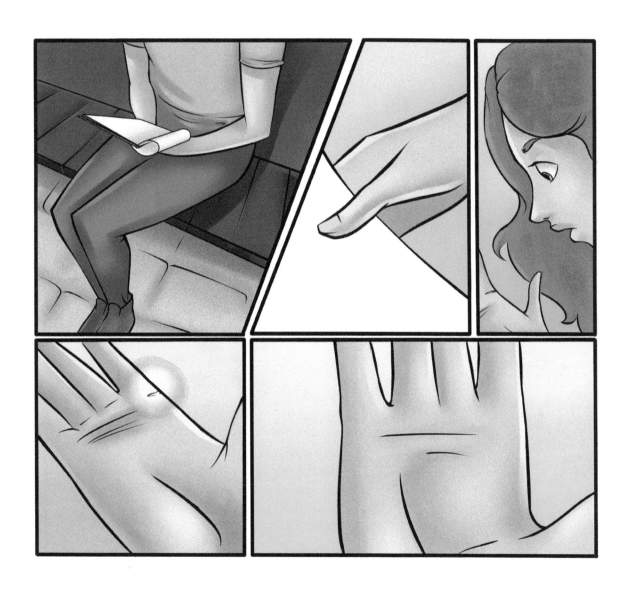

Letting out a sigh, Fenna closes her eyes again and thinks of the other Keepers. She opens her sketch pad and starts to create outfits for the other girls. “I know one of them is going to want a cape.”

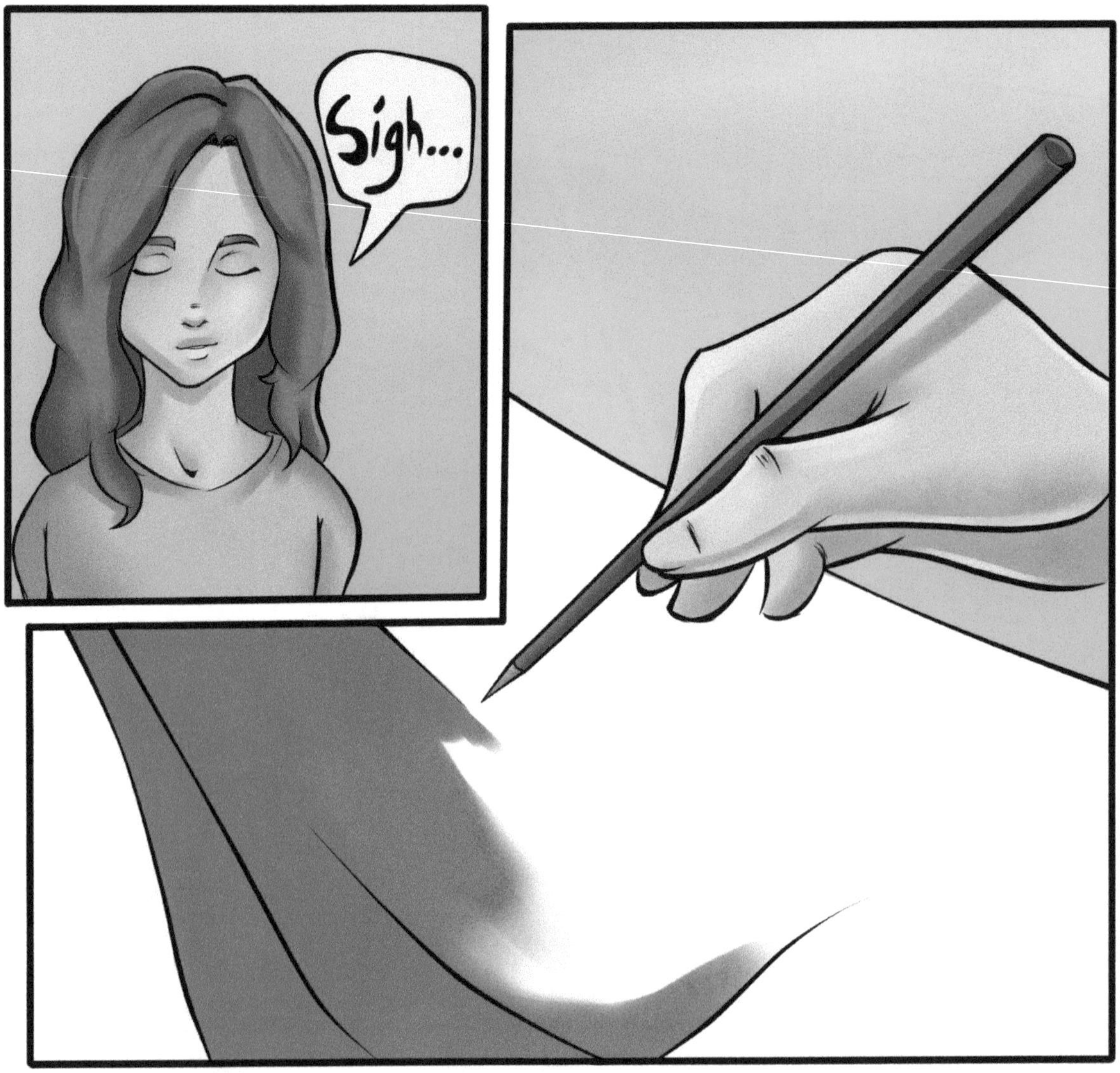
Sigh...

In the main library in Bogotá, Colombia, Ixchel walks to her favorite table with a stack of books. She grabs a geography book from the stack and puts her hand on top of it. As she uses her powers to read at superspeed, the pages begin to turn and suddenly stop on South Korea. "I wonder if any of The Keepers live there," Ixchel says.

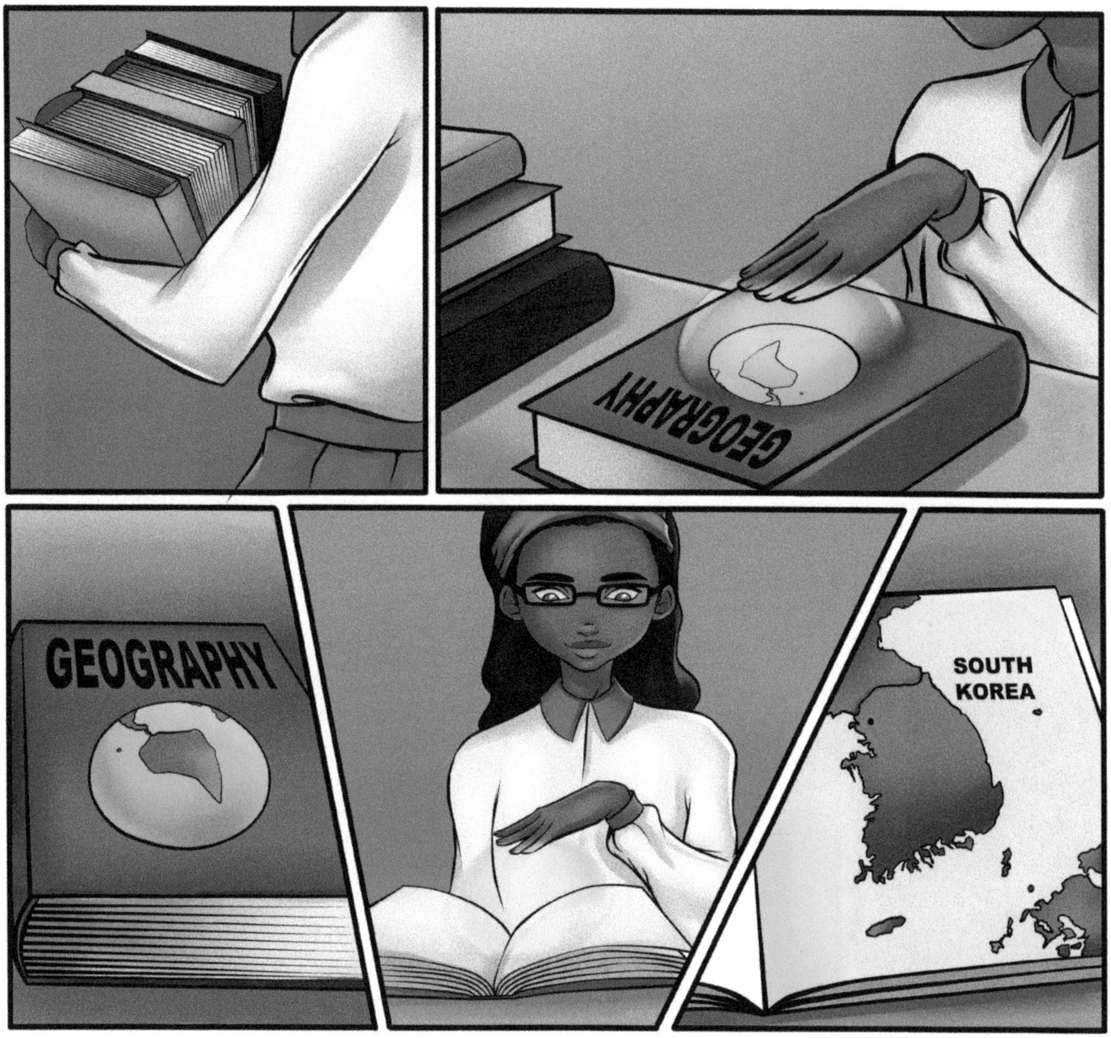

GEOGRAPHY
GEOGRAPHY
SOUTH KOREA

On the way to Earth from her home planet, Amaya discovered she had the power to travel through portals. She opened her first portal in Seoul, South Korea where she now lives.

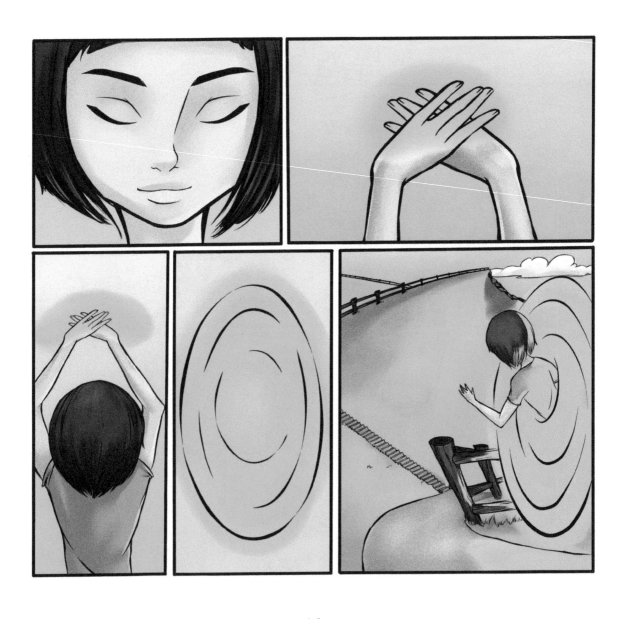

When Amaya learned to control her power, she began traveling all over the world to some amazing places.

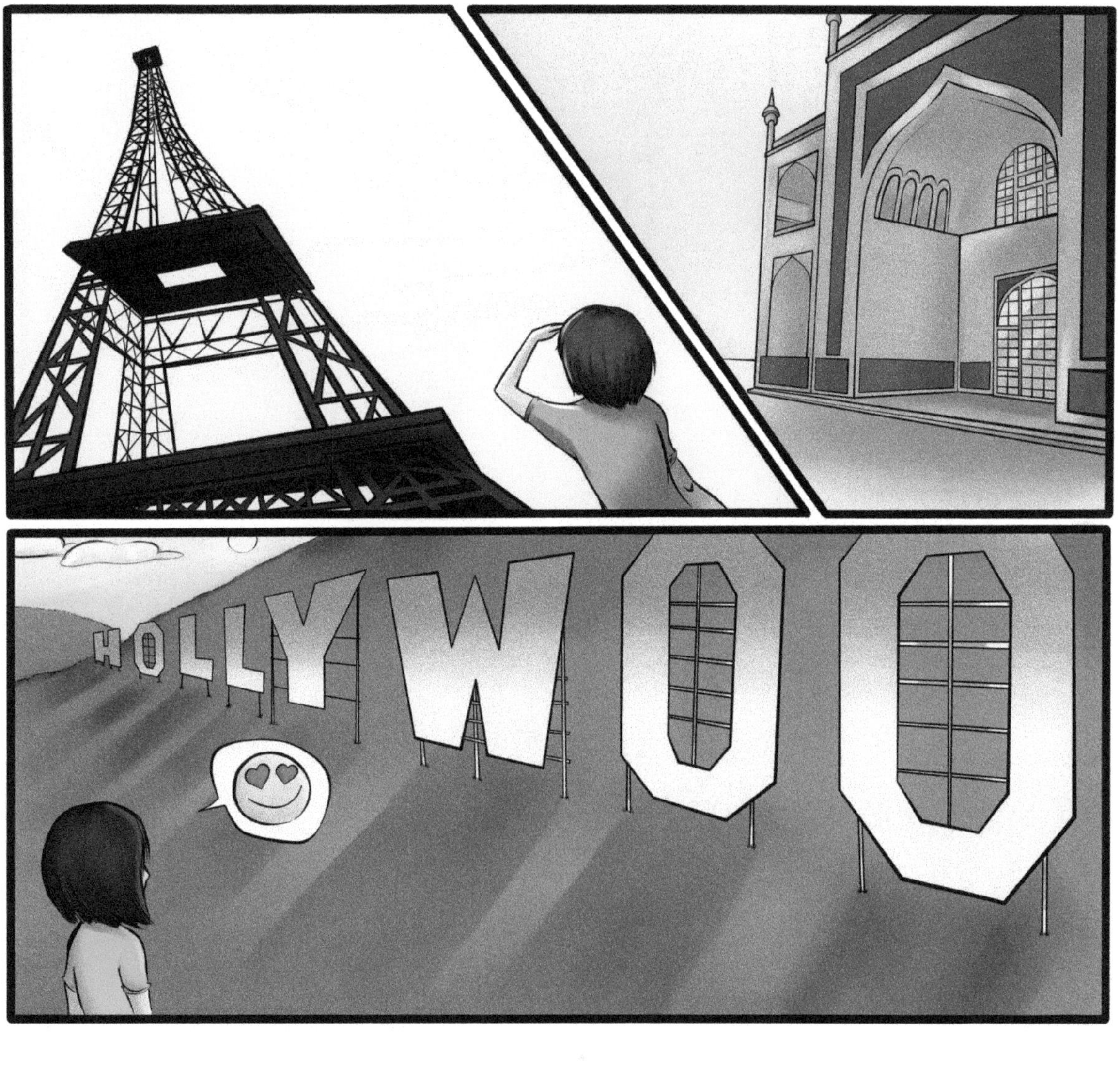
HOLLYWOO

As the oldest of the Keepers, Amaya wanted to make sure the other girls were safe. But she only knew where one of them lived.

On the beach of the Gullah Sea Islands in South Carolina, Kala skipped stones across the water. She knew she didn't have much time before she had to get back to her training.

As the future leader of the Keepers and a Princess, Kala knows she has to practice her powers everyday so she can be ready to lead her team.

After training with her Aunt Ife, Kala goes to her Aunt Katia to learn math, science, and other subjects. Kala knows that everything she learns will help her team be the best Keepers that they can be.

Later that evening, the girls looked up to see five "stars" glowing in the night sky. They all knew and understood their destiny but right now, Adanna, Amaya, Fenna, Ixchel and Kala would just enjoy being children with special powers.

AZA COMICS
THE KEEPERS
© 2014-2016 Aza Entertainment

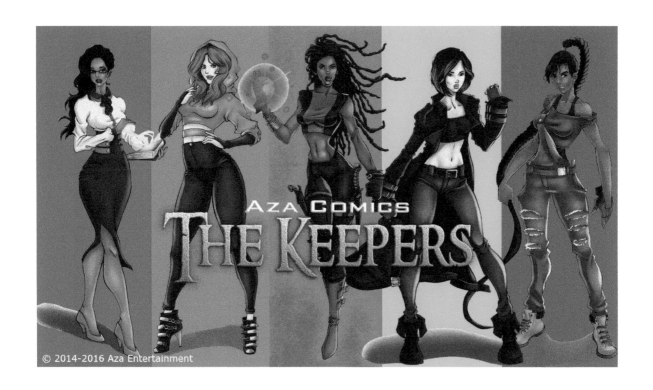

Are you ready to be a guardian?

Guardians keep the identities of The Keepers a secret and protect other kids from bullies.

Guardian Oath: I promise to keep the identity of The Keepers a secret so that Kiran cannot find them. I also promise to tell an adult if I see another kid being bullied. GOOOOOO AZA!

Welcome to Team Aza!

CPSIA information can be obtained
at www.ICGtesting.com
Printed in the USA
BVHW021630140720
583707BV00002B/38